GARDEN
OF THE
GOOD FOLK

by **Evelyn Foster**

Published by Country Books/Ashridge Press
in association with Spiral Publishing Ltd

Country Books, 38 Pulla Hill Drive
Storrington, West Sussex RH20 3LS

Tel: 07889 234 964
email: jonathan@spiralpublishing.com

www.storyteller.biz

ISBN 978-1-7395824-3-2

British Library Cataloguing in Publication Data.
A catalogue record for this book is available from the
British Library.

Printed and bound in England by 4edge Limited,
22 Eldon Way Industrial Estate, Hockley, Essex SS5 4AD

Dedication:

For my Mum:
who has always loved gardens.

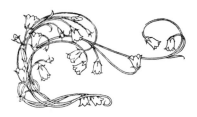

~ Evelyn Foster ~

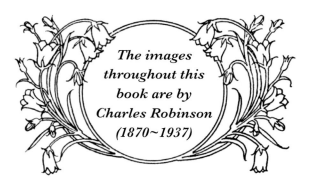

The images throughout this book are by Charles Robinson (1870~1937)

CHAPTER ONE

THE SECRET MESSAGE

E lfrida Green had a problem. She thought she might be an elf! This was an unusual thing to think.

But Elfrida was unusual. She lived in the countryside, and was small and delicate with a pointed nose and slanting green eyes.

"If only I could know for sure," thought Elfrida. So she wrote a message. She hid it under the secret squirrel statue in her garden.

The statue was so overgrown, it was very hard to see it. Only Elfrida knew it was there!

Elfrida's garden was her favourite place in the whole world. She had always thought it was magic. It had beds of bluebells, wildflower walks and mysterious hollow trees.

Dear Elves, (wrote Elfrida)

I'm writing to you because I think I might be an elf. I have a wand, I like milk and mice and I'm quite good at sewing. I also love dressing up as an elf and as an Edwardian girl. What do you think?

Love,

Elfrida

Elfrida left the message, then crossed her fingers. Would the elves reply?

That night, Elfrida could not sleep. She thought of all the things that could go wrong. A cat could find the message and eat it. A bird could find the message and fly off with it. Elfrida gave up trying to sleep, got up early and went to the garden.

What would she find?

Under the statue was a letter on green paper. Her garden *was* magic and the elves *had* replied!

~ CHAPTER TWO ~
THE PARTY

Dear Elfrida,

I am Elwin, head of all garden elves. It may well be you are an elf, especially if you like milk, mice and sewing. But to be sure, we need to know more about you. Do you like gardens? Do you dance in dew circles? True elves are fans of both gardens and the countryside.

By the way, humans do not always understand about dancing in dew circles. If caught by a human getting grass and mud everywhere, it is best to become invisible.

From Elwin

Elfrida was thrilled. There were fairy folk in her garden – actual elves!

Better than that, there was a chance she might be an elf. She wondered what would happen next.

What happened next was that Mimi Next Door came round. She had come to talk about the Magic Party she was holding for her birthday. Elfrida was going as an elf, Mimi as a fairy and Mimi's little sister, Rhiannon, was going as a gnome. If only, thought Elfrida, she could find out if she was an elf *before* the Magic Party.

As soon as Mimi had gone home, Elfrida watered her rose trees. Then she sent another message:

Dear Elwin,

I love living in the country, dancing in dew circles and helping in the garden. But Dad says elves pull weeds out, not flowers like I do.

Do you think he's right?

Love,

Elfrida

9

A few hours later, she found another magic message:

Dear Elfrida,

We were pleased to hear about the gardening. It sounds as if you might be an elf (don't worry about the weeds, even elves make mistakes.) But we need to know more. Can you do magic? If so, which kind?

If you grant love and joy to people, this means you are a good elf. Indeed true elves are often known as the Good Folk.

However, if you give them bad temper and spots, you are definitely a bad elf!

From Elwin

Elfrida was not sure. Could she do magic? Perhaps she could learn to work spells? But just before the party, something bad happened and Elfrida had no time to try.

Mimi's little sister, Rhiannon, spilt paint all over Mimi's fairy costume.

It looked like Mimi would be the only one without a costume at her own Magic Party!

~ CHAPTER THREE ~
THE COSTUME

Elfrida felt terrible. Then she had an idea. Elfrida searched in her wardrobe, and there it was: a Fairy Queen costume Mum had once made her for dressing up. Elfrida ran next door. She put the costume on the steps addressed to Mimi and left.

With any luck, Mimi would think it had been delivered by magic.

Elfrida was glad to have helped her friend, but she could not help feeling sad. If only she could have found out if she was an elf.

Yet it was just too late. Elfrida trudged, very slowly, home.

When she got home, there was a magic message for her:

Dear Elfrida,

By making good magic for your friend, you have shown you are one of us. Please fold this letter three times. By the way, if any human doesn't believe you are an elf, you can always bring them out in warts!

From Elwin

Elfrida was so happy! It had not been too late. She was an elf after all. She folded the letter three times and found herself flying through the air.

~ CHAPTER FOUR~
THE KINGDOM OF THE ELVES

E lfrida landed in the Kingdom of the Elves. It was a magical kingdom. The scents were sweeter, the shades sharper than those in the human world. Birds flew through gardens of beautiful flowers which swayed in a permanent breeze. Blossom-covered trees talked with plants, and bluebells and harebells played music.

Elwin, a wise-looking elf, came to meet her. He made

Elfrida an official Elf Friend and gave her a golden acorn ring. It was more than she had ever imagined!

Elfrida climbed trees with tree elves, rode stars with star elves and raced up and down rainbows with rain elves. When she got back, her clothes were shining with a magical elf light.

Better still, she arrived home only seconds after she'd left – thanks to the enchantment of the elves!

Then she went to Mimi's Magic Party.

There were fairy lights, bouncy castles, conjuring tricks and fairy cakes. Mimi wore Elfrida's costume and they both had a magical time. When they saw Elfrida's ring and the elf light on her clothes, her friends simply had to believe. So no warts were necessary.

At least, not yet ...!

~ CHAPTER FIVE ~
THE MERMAIDS

Three weeks later, Elfrida felt fed up. She was on holiday by the sea with Mum and Dad. Yet Elfrida missed her friends.

She missed Mimi from next door. She even missed Mimi's little sister, Rhiannon. Although Rhiannon had put toothpaste in her bed the last time they had a sleepover!

Elfrida could not help wishing some friends her own age were here to play with. Then she thought of something. As they were next to the sea, maybe mermaids would play with her?

"Wouldn't it be amazing," thought Elfrida; "if I could make friends with mermaids and get them to

play with me?" She would start by showing them she loved water. So, in the garden, in full view of the sea, Elfrida jumped in the paddling pool.

Water flew over the edge and splashed Dad who was sunbathing nearby!

Yet, nothing happened. Still, Elfrida's elf friend, Elwin, had showed her how she could keep in touch with him. So Elfrida wrote a message to Elwin asking for advice:

Dear Elwin,

I've been playing with water, though Dad was a bit cross when I got it all over him! Do you think mermaids will play with me?

Love,

Elfrida

She hid it under a stone in the garden of the house they were renting. Then a robin, a secret elf friend, took it to Elwin in Elfrida's magic garden back home.

Elfrida did
not hear back
for some time.
She thought
of all the things
that might have
gone wrong. The
robin might have
got lost. He might
have been mugged
by a bigger bird. But
next morning, the
robin landed safely
on her sill with a
message.

Elfrida patted
the robin's
head and then
opened
her letter.

~ CHAPTER SIX ~
THE LETTERS

Dear Elfrida,

Don't worry about the splashing. Even mermaids do that sometimes.

They also love fish of every kind. Why don't you go to the beach and see if you can find some? Good luck!

From Elwin

Elfrida asked Mum to take her to the beach.
Mum lay down to sunbathe and soon fell asleep. Elfrida saw some fish in a rock pool. She

talked to them and stroked their scales. But still she did not see a mermaid. She was starting to think she would *never* see one. So when she got back, she wrote to Elwin:

Dear Elwin,

I still haven't seen any mermaids or got them to play with me. Is there anything else I could do? Please help!

Love,

Elfrida

The robin soon brought a magic message from Elwin:

Dear Elfrida,

Mermaids are shy, but why don't you try again? They like combing their hair. They are also good at singing. You could try this, but not too loudly as humans get annoyed if you smash the light bulbs!

From Elwin

Elfrida spent ages combing her hair. Mum and Dad could not believe it! Elfrida usually hated combing her hair. Next, she sang a song (not too loudly). Then she begged Dad to take her to the beach.

Dad lay down to sunbathe, while Elfrida eagerly scanned the sea. Suddenly, she saw something. Could it be a mermaid at last?

~ CHAPTER SEVEN ~
THE KINGDOM OF THE MERMAIDS

It was just some plastic someone had thrown away. Elfrida sighed. She had to accept it. She was *never* going to meet a mermaid. Still, she took all the plastic out of the waves so sea creatures would not get caught up in it.

Moments later, there came a great flash of light and two beautiful mermaids appeared!

"I am Aria and this is Alina," said the first mermaid. "You have helped save sea creatures from choking, and you have helped us too. Now we know you are a true mermaid friend. Come and play with us!" Elfrida went red with delight.

The second mermaid waved a gentle sleeping

spell over Dad and an underwater breathing spell over Elfrida.

All three of them dived into the sea. Then the mermaids took Elfrida to a magical underwater garden. It had coral paths, sparkling stones and flowers that could never fade. Bushes swayed in an underwater breeze and seaweed gave forth light.

Then Elfrida and the mermaids played together. They raced dolphins and seahorses. The mermaids showed Elfrida their secret caves and the hidden treasures of the deep. It was one of the most wonderful days of her life! When Elfrida got home, she wrote to Elwin and told him all about it.

Elfrida was never lonely after that, even when her friends were not around. Because even when she could not get to the beach, mermaids popped up in her paddling pool – and talked and played with her!

~ CHAPTER EIGHT ~
THE MAGIC HOUSE

One day, Elfrida thought up something exciting to do. She would make a Magic House in her garden. She now called her garden *The Garden of the Good Folk* – thanks to all the magic beings who were there!

First, with Dad's help, she made a shelter from wood and bracken. Then she made a table from a box. She made a small bed and chair, and added books, fairy ornaments, lanterns and games. At last, she had her very own Magic House. Now all she needed was someone magic to stay in it!

A few days later, Elfrida saw someone in her Magic House.

It was a tiny girl with white wings and a shiny wand and crown.

"Who are you?" Elfrida cried.

"I'm Celeste, a fairy princess from the kingdom of Fallias," the tiny girl replied.

"I wandered into the mortal world by mistake, and now I can't get home! My travel spells don't seem to work in this world."

"You can stay in my Magic House," said Elfrida.

Celeste thanked her and settled down in Elfrida's Magic House.

She drank juice from Elfrida's doll's tea set and she and Elfrida played together.

While her visitor was resting, Elfrida weeded her tulip beds.

Then she wrote to Elwin:

Dear Elwin,

A fairy princess called Celeste is here and she needs to get back to her kingdom. Can you tell me how to help her?

Thank you!

Love,

Elfrida

She left the message in her secret place in the garden.

Elfrida soon got a reply:

Dear Elfrida,

Yes, we can help her, but first we must find out if she is a true princess and not a Bad Elf in disguise. This will not require magic, but good detective work. True fairy princesses usually have very soft skin. The sort that can feel a pea through many mattresses. They are also very good at getting lost.

From Elwin

Well, thought Elfrida, Celeste was already lost, but what about her skin? There was only one way to find out!

~ CHAPTER NINE ~
THE FAIRY PRINCESS

E lfrida picked a single pea from a pod in the vegetable patch.

She loved helping Mum and Dad grow fruit and vegetables, as well as flowers, in the garden. She then ran to her Magic House. She was so excited she tripped over and nearly ended up in a lilac bush!

While Celeste was eating, Elfrida slipped the pea under the mattress. Now all she had to do was wait. Would Celeste turn out to be a visiting princess or a Bad Elf in disguise?

Next morning, Elfrida ran to her Magic House. "How did you sleep?" she asked Celeste.

"Miserably!" groaned Celeste. "I'm black and blue all over."

Elfrida felt a surge of relief – though she felt a bit guilty too!

Then, over the fence, she saw Rhiannon, little sister of Mimi Next Door. She was wearing a tiara and holding a wand.

"I'm being a Princess," said Rhiannon, proudly.

"Well, you look great," said Elfrida, and went in to write a message:

Dear Elwin,

I put the pea under Celeste's mattress and she hardly slept at all.

Love,

Elfrida

A short time later, Elwin replied:

Dear Elfrida,

This sounds hopeful. Celeste may be a genuine princess.

Yet we need to be sure. Bad elves can be very crafty, so be careful, whatever you do.

True princesses mostly love apples: especially when offered by a queen in disguise. Be very careful.

From Elwin

Elfrida shivered. Could Celeste be a Bad Elf after all?

~ CHAPTER TEN ~
THE CRYSTAL CASTLE

E lfrida got an apple. Yet before she could give it to Celeste, she saw Rhiannon again. This time, Rhiannon was in tears.

"My princess wand," sobbed Rhiannon. "I broke it!"

Elfrida felt very sorry for her.

"I'll see what I can do," she promised.

Indoors, Elfrida searched but could not find her spare wand.

She was so worried about Rhiannon, she ran outside: nearly tripping over again. Yet Rhiannon was smiling and in her hand was a wand.

"It was pushed under the fence with my name

on it," beamed Rhiannon. By her feet, where Rhiannon could not see, Celeste winked at her.

Elfrida winked back and went off to write a letter:

Dear Elwin,

Celeste conjured up a play wand for Rhiannon when Rhiannon broke hers. What do you think?

Love,

Elfrida

A reply came half an hour later:

Elfrida, no further proof is necessary. The one thing we know for sure about a princess is that she has a golden heart. If you work this travel spell, only known to garden elves, it will take this princess home.

Elfrida said the secret spell. Then she and Celeste were flying.

The spell flew them to the crystal castle of Fallias. The walls of the castle shone and shimmered. There

39

was food on glimmering tables and
drink in glistening goblets.
Flowers bloomed from
exquisite vases and minstrels
played magical music.

"Come and eat with me,"
Celeste said to Elfrida; "as you are an
elf and a true elf friend, fairy food
will not harm you."

So Elfrida and Celeste feasted,
while outside, trees clicked their twigs
in time to the music and hedgehogs
did a line dance!

After the feast, they all went out into
the palace grounds. The grounds had hedges in the
shape of unicorns and paths that were paved with
pearls. Silver fountains sprang up, dazzlingly, from
the ground.

A firework party was held for Elfrida. Wizards
worked wonderful spells while fireworks filled the air.

"What are you thinking?" Celeste asked her as they watched the fireworks together. Elfrida smiled.

"I'm thinking," she answered: "I can hardly wait for my next adventure."

As the fireworks soared, Elfrida had a feeling she would not have long to wait ....!

~ CHAPTER ELEVEN ~
THE NEXT ADVENTURE

E lfrida was having a picnic lunch in the garden when she found a message from Elwin. This was quite unusual. Elfrida usually wrote to him first. What could Elwin want? There was only one way to find out! Elfrida opened the secret message and read it:

Dear Elfrida, (wrote Elwin)

We, the elves, need your help on a quest.

If you are willing to help us, pick a leaf from the red rose bush. It will take you to me.

From Elwin

Elfrida's first reaction was to panic. *Could* she help? But then, she thought, she had already proved she was a friend to elves and mermaids and a rescuer of princesses. She could do this, she really could. Or, at least, she could try!

Elfrida took a deep breath. She picked a leaf from the bush and put it in her pocket. The garden started to shake. Then a cloud came and swept her

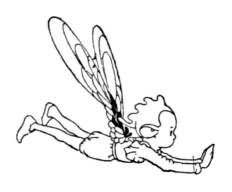

away. Seconds later, to her delight, she was standing beside Elwin in a cool green forest.

"What is this quest, Elwin?" she asked him.

Elwin looked at her, gravely.

"Long ago," he told her; "Bright Court Elves left this world as the time of the humans had come. There are only three left, and it is now time for them to return to Elfland. Yet the Bad Elves, the Dockalfar, have cast a sleep spell on one of them, so that she cannot return. Only a true elf friend like you can undo Evil Spells in *this* world. Will you help us?"

"I will!" Elfrida replied at once.

Elwin bowed in gratitude.

"Then come with me," he said.

45

~ CHAPTER TWELVE ~
THE MAGICAL MOUNTAINS

Elwin whirled into the air and Elfrida whirled with him. They arrived in a range of mountains. At once, it began to snow.

Elfrida felt sure the snow had been sent by the Bad Elves.

She could feel harsh, unfriendly eyes on the back of her neck.

But when she looked, no-one was there.

Elwin began to walk and Elfrida followed him. They had walked for about ten minutes when Elfrida heard it.

"Look out!" she yelled.

Down down from the hills it came: an avalanche

roaring like a dragon. Even above the noise it made, Elfrida could hear cruel elven laughter. With a shout, she dragged Elwin out of the way and flung herself down beside him. Then she put her hands over her ears.

Down came the avalanche until it landed on the spot where they had stood. If they had still been standing there, they would have been swept away! Yet the cruel elven laughter had been silenced.

When they had recovered, Elwin led her on to the heart of the mountains to the frozen mouth of an ice cave.

It was snowing so thickly now it was hard to see properly. Yet Elwin began to sing in a low bell-like voice. As he sang, the frost cover melted, revealing a long tunnel. Elwin hurried inside it. The tunnel was as dark as the cupboard under the stairs Elfrida had once got stuck in. She really did not want to go in there. But she knew she must for the sake of the quest.

Clenching her fists, Elfrida went in.

~ CHAPTER THIRTEEN ~
THE HIDDEN CAVE

The air of the tunnel seemed to press down on her. It was almost totally dark. Gritting her teeth, Elfrida stumbled on. Then, suddenly, she remembered … she had a pocket torch!

Fumbling in her pocket, Elfrida found it. Once it was on, the tunnel looked less scary. She could now make out plants flowering in the walls: hazel, flame flower and holly. Elfrida looked at them with pleasure. She really loved plants.

Then she heard Elwin gasp, and

hurried to join him. The tunnel had come out in a cave. It was huge and full of shadows. There were flaming torches on the walls, but they did not shed much light.

Suddenly, the floor cracked open!

Elfrida screamed. Was this some new trick of the Dockalfar?

Up through the floor rose a marble bench. As it came, more shadows flickered on the walls: of birds and horses, trees and flowers, elven lords and silk-clad ladies. Then the shadows faded and the bench lay still.

A figure lay upon it. Elfrida clutched Elwin in delight. They had found the enchanted Elf! She had green hair, pale features and she was deeply asleep.

Then Elfrida's pulse leapt. The chamber had started to shudder.

"What is it?" she cried.

Elwin's face was grim.

"It is the Dockalfar," he said. "They are destroying the chamber. If you cannot wake the Elf, we will be buried alive!"

Elfrida stared at him in horror.

"But how do we wake her?"

"I may not help you," said Elwin, grimly.

"Only an elf from the human world can decide."

Rock and earth showered down from the walls. A knot of dread tightened inside Elfrida. What power could she possibly have that was strong enough to save both their lives? Her mind desperately twisted and turned, trying to find an answer.

She thought of them coming through the tunnel and of the plants in the walls. She thought of her great love of plants and all that Elwin and her reading had taught her. Suddenly, she remembered that in the magic realms, hazel was a health-giving plant and that holly was proof against evil. Perhaps something inside her might save them after all. Perhaps her love of gardens and plants?

Elfrida ran back. She cut some hazel and holly and raced back again. At top speed, she wove the plants into a crown and placed it on the Elf's head. She pricked her finger and one drop of blood fell onto the Elf's waxen face. Elfrida waited, hardly daring to breathe.

The Elf did not stir. It had not worked!

Elfrida felt sick to her soul.

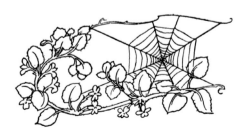

~ CHAPTER FOURTEEN ~
THE FIELDS OF THE CLOUDS

T hen, something surprising happened. A warm red blush appeared on the Elf's pale cheek. Her smooth eyelids flickered. She opened her eyes and looked straight at Elfrida. Her eyes were the colour of emeralds.

The next instant, the shuddering in the cave stopped. There was a terrible howl of rage and then silence.

Slowly, the High Court Elf sat up. As Elfrida stood, awestruck, the Elf gazed at her. She seemed to be reading her mind. At last, her face lightened and she smiled at Elfrida.

"The Dockalfar are destroyed. We are all in your

debt and I am going home!"
she cried.

Elfrida let out a sigh of
relief. Elwin laid a gentle
hand on her shoulder. "You
are a true elven hero!" he
said. Then he flew them, all
three, to the Kingdom of the
Elves.

Magical flowers sprinkled
dew over Elfrida's dress and it
turned into a green velvet ballgown.

Elwin and Elfrida returned the High Court Elf to
her people. Then the elves held a Grand Court Ball
for them.

"Thank you, Elfrida, our half-human sister!"
they cried.

They pulled her, laughing, into a palace with
a roof made of rainbows. Elfrida danced with
elves and fairy princes in a brilliant ballroom.

Glowworms glittered like stars on the walls and butterflies waltzed overhead.

After midnight, Elwin flew her home again. He promised to keep in touch, and said that elves would always watch over her.

Better still, he said she could return to them whenever she wished it.

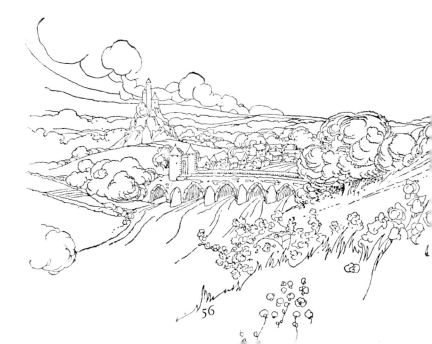

So some nights, when the moon is bright, Elfrida flies through the skies with Elwin. Then they dance together in the beautiful ballroom in the Secret Kingdom of the Elves!

57

~ CHAPTER FIFTEEN ~
ELWIN'S INSIDE GUIDE TO ELVES

D o you think *you* might be an elf or a true elf friend? Read Elwin's Inside Guide and find out for sure!

A TENDENCY TO SHORTNESS

Although elves vary to some degree, they are usually quite small. This is, of course, why they are known as the Little People. So if you are the sort of person who has to stand on a chair to reach a shelf or sink, you may be an elf or an elf friend.

A CURIOUS RELATIONSHIP WITH TIME

Magic time is different from ours as Little People have their own time frame. This is why it is a serious thing to have a sleepover with an elf. When you come back, you may find either that you're back before you left, or that several years have gone by. Those who do not own a watch or are often late may well be elves in disguise!

A PASSION FOR QUESTS

Do you have a thing about quests?

As soon as you hear there is a magic ring to be destroyed, or a Dark Lord to be defeated, do you rush off at once to help?

If you do all this, instead of running in the opposite direction, you are probably an elf.

Special Elf Note: When embarking on a quest, it is usually a good idea to take some hobbits and heroes along.

A GOOD RELATIONSHIP WITH KINGS, QUEENS AND PRINCESSES

Elves also tend to get on well with Kings, Queens and Fairy Princesses. So if you are friendly with any Kings, Queens or Fairy Princesses, this could mean you are an elf or a true elf friend.

A GOOD RELATIONSHIP WITH FATHER CHRISTMAS

Having a close friendship with Father Christmas means you may be a *Christmas* elf. If you live at the North Pole and are good at making toys, then you are almost bound to be one.

Christmas elves are hard-working and like to make many things: but they like making toys most of all.

BEING GOOD AT SEWING AND MAKING SHOES

Elves are also good at sewing and making shoes. They are particularly keen to help shoemakers.

So if you are good at sewing, or make shoes in the middle of the night, you are likely to be an elf or elf friend. An ability to spin straw into gold is also an advantage.

A true elf knows exactly what shoes are wanted and by whom.

Cinderella, of course, will only wear glass slippers, while Puss in Boots is famous for his stylish boots.

Elves themselves like long thin shoes with very pointy toes.

A PASSION FOR POTIONS

All elves love lotions and potions and can't resist making them.

Elves make magic potions at all times of year. So if you love cooking and making things in the kitchen, there is a fair chance *you* may be an elf.

Elf Tip 1: It might be best to admit to anyone in the kitchen that you are an elf. Otherwise they may get a bit cross when you produce a wart potion – instead of those pancakes you were meant to be making.

Elf Tip 2: Anyone with warts, though, will be seriously impressed!

A LIKING FOR REINDEER AND OTHER ANIMALS

All elves love animals and are always kind to them. This is one of the many reasons why people call them The Good Folk.

They have a special liking for mice who are their particular friends.

They are also attached to horses. All magic creatures know that horses are lucky, which is why the horseshoe is a symbol of good luck. So if you love riding or help out in a stable, you may be an elf or a true elf friend.

Special Note 1: A passion for winged horses and unicorns is particularly useful.

Special Note 2: Elves know that beneath every frog or beast, a friend or handsome prince may be lurking.

A FEELING FOR MAGIC

If you can do magic and have a magic wand, you are probably an elf. Wands are useful for casting spells and for defeating evil. They can also be disguised as staffs: very handy on a quest.

If you are the sort of person who goes round granting love, riches and happiness with your wand, you are a good elf or *liosalfar*. If however, you wish people grief, hardship and bad luck, you are a bad elf or *dockalfar*. Anyone who works magic for a friend is the very best elf there can be!

A LOVE OF THE COLOUR GREEN

Green has long been the colour of magic, and all self-respecting elves wear it. Elves love rich green material and sport smart green jackets. More down-to-earth elves wear hotpants: with natty green stockings or tights.

The High Court Elves, on the other hand, wear flowing robes in a Medieval style. These green and silver robes are made of silk or lace. But elven clothes, for the *really* discerning, are woven from mist and from moonlight!

So if you find yourself wearing enchanting green clothes, you may be an elf or a true elf friend.

Elf Tip: Some humans do not understand about elf fashion. So if they give you a hard time about what you wear, don't worry – it is all part of being an elf.

A TASTE FOR RED

Elves also love red: another shade linked to magic. Christmas elves, in particular, like to wear red dungarees and caps. Some elf caps are long, like nightcaps or hoods, with a tassel on the end. Others are shorter and worn close to the head.

Special Note: A liking for unusual jewellery is also an advantage.

A LIKING FOR MUSIC

All elves love music. So if you are a musician
or mad about music, you may well be an elf in
disguise. Elf music is enchanting, beautiful and
mostly a source of good.

All elves sing wonderfully in otherworldly voices.
Elf music is often played in
forests where it appears to be
coming from the trees. So
if you love singing in your
room, in a choir or a forest,
there's a good chance
you may be an elf.

A LOVE OF DANCE

Elves are also mad about dancing. It is one of their
chosen pursuits. Elves prefer to dance in glades as
there is less chance of humans spotting them. So if
you love dancing to music outside, you may well be
an elf or a true elf friend.

Special Elf Note: It is worth noting here that most humans do not understand about dancing outside, and get annoyed if you tread grass in the house. If caught by a human getting grass and mud everywhere, it is best to become invisible!

Special Elf Warning: It is a good idea to avoid the dance known as 'the Elf King's Tune.' Once this is played, fiddlers cannot stop playing and dancers cannot stop dancing.

This can become inconvenient.

A LOVE OF THE OUTDOORS

Elves are mad about nature and are very close to
it. They are usually to be found in wild areas or
mysteriously hollow hills.

Elves also like to live in woodlands. They live in
treehouses or have homes inside hollow tree trunks
or hills. So if you are someone who has a treehouse,
you may well be an elf or an elf friend.

High Elves live in a special land of their own known as Elfland. This is a part of fairyland inhabited only by elves.

Elfland is a land of spring, filled with beautiful plants, which sway in a permanent breeze.

A HEAD FOR MOUNTAINS

The great mountains of the world are also said to house elves.

The caves found in mountains are thought to hide a number of elven homes. The Norse word for elf, *alf*, is thought by some to come from the word for mountains: *Alps*.

The winter elves, the elves of frost, ice and snow, all live in the mountains and need a good head for heights.

So if you are a mountaineer, a skier or just love

climbing, you may well be an elf or a true elf friend.

Elf mountain homes are, of course, very high up, so you have to be fit to get there. In fact, most elves are fit. This is because they may need to flee from a giant or a dragon. They also need to be able to climb trees and rush about on quests.

Special Note 1: Anyone suffering from a fear of heights is unlikely to be a mountain elf.

Special Note 2: Any fan of any of the *Frozen* films is, however, likely to be one!

A GREAT LOVE OF GARDENS

Elves love gardens more than anything and know about plants and flowers. Indeed true elves are interested in plants, herbs and flowers from the earliest age. They use them in spells to make people happy and to heal heroes when they are sick.

So if you love gardening and growing flowers and herbs, you may well be an elf. Anyone who has their own watering can is almost bound to be one.

Special Tip 1: If you go out in the garden a lot, it is best to keep away from nettles.

Special Tip 2: Being careful around thistles is also a very good idea.

AN ABILITY TO LIVE FOREVER

Elves live for hundreds of years. Indeed they claim to be the Elder Race: the first of all known beings. If able to keep away from villains, they often live forever. So if you feel you have lived a long time, you are almost certainly an elf.

Whenever this feeling grows too strong, true elves depart into the West. So if you often go on holiday to the west, this may mean you are an elf or a true elf friend.

A LIKING FOR FOOD AND DRINK

Elves love food and drink: especially bread, honey, milk and strawberries. So if you love any of the above foods, you may be an elf or an elf friend.

Elves hold great parties in forests, where there is music, dancing till dawn and plenty to eat and

drink. Elves also make a
foodstuff called lembas.
This consists of dry
wafers which last an
incredibly long time.
They are useful to take on
quests and are not very tasty.

They do give you lots of
energy though.

KEEPING YOUR PROMISES

An elf always keeps their promises. Whether they
are made to a friend, enemy, wizard or family
member, the principle remains the same. The best
elves do always keep their word – even between
gritted teeth!

Elf Tip: It is best to remain cheerful when keeping
a difficult yet noble promise. This is hard, but true
elves can do it.

A LOVE OF STORIES

All elves love stories. They know that to be an elf it helps to be wise and that wisdom is found in books. Anyone who is always reading books is probably an elf. The more piles of books you have, and the more often the piles fall over, the more likely it is you are an elf or a true elf friend.

Elf Tip: Going to libraries and bookshops are good things for true elves to do.

NAMES AND TITLES

If you are a Lord, Lady, King or Queen, you have a high chance of being a High Elf. High Elves are aristocratic and tend to rejoice in titles.

High Court Elves, the relatives of the Bright Court Elves, are the most powerful elves of all.

If you are called Arwen, Galadriel, Celeborn or Elrond, you are certainly a High Elf.

Elf Tip 1: It is always best to keep your distance from anyone with names like Gollum, Rumplestiltskin or Sauron.

Elf Tip 2: Beings with names like Elwin, Elfrida, Gandalf or Celeste can, however, be trusted.

~ CONCLUSION ~

If you fit most of the guidelines above, then you are a true elf or a true elf friend. Being an elf or a true elf friend can be extremely exciting.

However, it is, above all, private. The secret is yours alone.

And, remember, if anybody doubts you … you can always bring them out in warts!

~ END ~

~ ABOUT EVELYN ~

Evelyn Foster was brought up in Essex where she saw many marvellous gardens.

She has worked as author, storyteller and actress, has spoken on fairytales at the Royal Festival Hall and appeared in fantasy art as a dryad. She has read to the blind, performed plays in parks and run myth and drama workshops at the British Museum.

Evelyn's books are mostly about elves, giants and mermaids. She has not yet met an elf, a giant or a mermaid … but she lives in hope!

~ OTHER BOOKS BY EVELYN ~

Include:

Frozen Fairytales for all Ages
(Country Books)

The Elves and the Trendy Shoes
For Children 4-7
(Hopscotch Twisty Tales)

For very young children:

Alan and the Animals
(Hachette)

And for grown-ups:

Land of Hope and Story
(Country Books)